D0343767

BALLOON

For Judy and Larry

First published in Great Britain by HarperCollins Publishers Ltd in 1998.

ISBN: 0 00 198218-4

1 3 5 7 9 10 8 6 4 2

Printed and bound in Singapore by Imago.

BALLOON

Jez Alborough

Collins

An Imprint of HarperCollins*Publishers*

Billy saw it

Mummy bought it

Man threw it

Billy caught it.

Billy pulled it and waved it

Billy headed

and saved it.

Billy squeezed it

Billy tossed it

Billy missed it and lost it.

Mummy saw it

Mummy chased it

Dog barked

Dog raced it.

Dog jumped   Dog whacked it

Duck quacked...

and attacked it.

Cow licked it   Cow flicked it

Cow mooed and Cow kicked it.

Bird flipped it

and flapped it   Tree tangled   and trapped it.

Wind threw it

Wind caught it

Wind blew it　　and...

...brought it.

Billy chased it

Billy...

...stopped it.

But tripped up

and...

popped it.

Mummy sighed, Dog looked glum, Billy saw...

another one!